The Cup of Ankh

randomhouse.com/kids

ISBN: 978-0-307-93141-2

Printed in the United States of America

10 9 8 7 6 5 4 3 2 1

nickelodeon™

HOUSE OF ANUBIS™

The Cup of Ankh

Adapted by Peter McGrath

Based on the script by Hans Bourlon,
Gert Verhulst, and Anjali Taneja

Random House  New York

PROLOGUE

Dear Diary,

I'm halfway through the first semester at my new boarding school in England, and already so much has happened! First a student named Joy disappeared from the residence I live in, Anubis House. Then an old lady named Sarah Frobisher-Smythe told me I'm the key to solving an ancient mystery and gave me an eye-shaped locket that can open secret doors and passageways in the house. Soon after, I discovered that Anubis House was built by Sarah's parents, who were accused of stealing treasure from King Tutankhamen's tomb. One item that was taken from the tomb was the Cup of Ankh—an Egyptian relic that enables anyone who drinks the Elixir of Life from it to live forever.

I'm not sure if the Cup of Ankh really exists, but with the help of Sarah and my friends, I have uncovered five puzzle pieces that could be Egyptian relics, and a bunch of clues that seem to lead to more clues—and perhaps more relics! My friends Fabian,

Amber, Patricia, and I have formed a secret club called Sibuna that's dedicated to solving the mystery of Anubis House.

We're not the only ones, though. Our creepy house guardian, Victor, seems to be part of some secret society that is also looking for the Cup of Ankh. There's a really scary guy named Rufus too. He seems to know about the Cup, and he keeps showing up in the weirdest places.

I hope we solve the mystery soon. The school prom is coming up in a few weeks, and I want to be free of all the house drama by then so I can concentrate on my personal life. I really hope Fabian asks me to the dance. . . .

1

Pale moonlight shone down on England's top boarding school. In Anubis House, where eight students lived, an American girl with light brown hair named Nina sat on a leather couch next to her friend Fabian. They had just come back to the house after performing in a school play and were discussing the day's events. After months of finding clues and puzzle pieces hidden in Anubis House, Nina had discovered a fourth puzzle piece hidden in the staircase. Before she could hide it again, their house guardian, Victor, showed up and quickly confiscated it, then locked it into a safe in his office. During the school play, Nina had managed to run back to Anubis House, open Victor's safe, and retrieve her puzzle piece, but she was stunned to find a fifth puzzle piece there as well.

"So Victor had another puzzle piece in his safe the whole time?" asked dark-haired Fabian in a low voice, looking over his shoulder to make sure Victor wasn't around.

"Yes!" Nina replied. "And he was really surprised when he found out there were two of them. I overheard him say there should only be 'one true relic.' What happens if there are more than the five we have?"

Nina and Fabian were interrupted by Victor, who strode in and beckoned to them. "You two. Come with me."

Nina glanced nervously at Fabian and followed Victor up to his office. Patricia and Amber were already there. Patricia was pacing. Her brown eyes flashed as she angrily demanded that Victor explain the disappearance of her best friend, Joy. Joy had unexpectedly shown up in the audience during the play but had fled after the curtain call. Patricia had seen Victor chase after her and knew he was somehow involved in her disappearance. "I want to know the truth!" she shouted.

Victor went to his computer. "You want to know the truth? I will show you the truth." He turned on his computer and spun the monitor around to face the students.

"Patricia?" said a voice from the screen.

Patricia gasped. She couldn't believe her eyes. Joy was looking at her via a webcam.

Patricia leaned toward the screen. "Joy! I came to find you after the play, but you were gone!"

"They wouldn't let me meet you. Said it was too dangerous," said Joy.

"Hey, it's okay. It's not your fault. When are you coming back?" Patricia asked.

"I'm not," said Joy sadly. "My dad works for the government. He has access to some top-secret documents. I can't say too much, but he says someone is after my family, so we've had to move away and change our names. It's just not safe for me to be at school anymore."

A man with silver-streaked hair entered the webcam picture. "Off the camera now, please, princess," Joy's dad said gently.

Joy looked at the Anubis House students. "Guys, I have to go. But listen, Victor and the teachers are protecting me. You should trust them." Her eyes filled with tears as she left the room.

"Happy now?" said Victor, looking coldly at Patricia. "Oh—and one more thing. From now on, you are all to go straight to school and then directly back to the house afterward. None of you goes anywhere without my knowledge."

The house guardian watched the students as they headed downstairs. "Do you think they bought it?" Joy's dad asked Victor.

"Yes," said Victor. He stroked his beard. "But I don't think we should allow them any more contact with Joy. We don't want anything to distract the Chosen One from fulfilling her destiny, now, do we?"

2

Nina and Fabian lingered over their scrambled eggs the next morning until the other Anubis House students had left. Only when they were alone did Fabian open up about his suspicions of Victor. "I know Joy said Victor was one of the good guys, but I still don't trust him," he confided. "He will look for the puzzle pieces once he discovers they're missing from his safe. I'm going to carry them in my backpack for safekeeping from now on."

Nina nodded. "That's a great idea."

As they were clearing their plates, their house mom, Trudy, hurried into the dining room and thrust a stack of envelopes into Fabian's hands. "I'm in a rush. Can you pass these on to Victor?" she asked cheerily.

As Trudy bustled off, Fabian glanced down and

whitened. "It's a toxicology report from the hospital," he whispered, singling out one of the envelopes. A few days before, their housemate Alfie had accidentally drunk a liquid that was possibly the Elixir of Life. He had started choking and convulsing, and had to spend a few days in the hospital.

Nina and Fabian dashed to find Amber and Patricia and call a Sibuna meeting. It was the Sibuna members who had discovered the Elixir in the basement of the house. They thought Victor had been drinking it and was actually more than a century old.

When Sibuna had gathered, Fabian read the toxicology report. "A mixture of . . . water, ginseng, angelica, and cinnamon bark. It's an herbal concoction. Says here that Alfie is allergic to one or more of the ingredients."

"It's not the Elixir of Life, then?" said Nina, crestfallen.

"So—Victor isn't over a hundred years old, and there is no Elixir," said Amber.

"And there's no mystery," Patricia added.

Nina frowned. "But none of it adds up. Just because there's no Elixir of Life doesn't mean there isn't a mystery to be solved! Guys, you're not giving up on me, are you?" she asked, though she already knew the answer.

Nina was distracted in class all day. Sibuna had come to a dead end with the Elixir theory, but there were still five strange puzzle pieces that had no explanation. What was more, Nina had had a dream that she couldn't shake off. She decided to tell Fabian about it as they walked back to Anubis House after school.

"Sarah appeared and kept saying 'Eleven. Zero one. One nine. One five,'" Nina said. "I think she was trying to give me a hint about solving the next clue. What do those numbers mean?"

Fabian wasn't paying attention. Finally, he blurted out, "I've sort of misplaced one of the puzzle pieces."

"What?" Nina said loudly. Fabian lowered his head and told Nina he had hidden his backpack, with the puzzle pieces inside, on top of his locker. "I thought there was going to be a bag search, so I hid it," he explained. "One of the pieces must have fallen out. I looked all around for it as soon as I realized it was missing, but I couldn't find it. It could have been swept up by the janitor."

Nina paled. "Or Victor could have found it!"

The two glumly entered Anubis House. In the living room, Patricia greeted them with a twinkle in her eye. "Lost something?" she laughed, bringing the missing puzzle piece into view.

Fabian gasped. "Where did you find it?"

Patricia explained that she had taken it from Alfie. Alfie had found the puzzle piece at school, next to Fabian's locker. Alfie was a huge believer in UFOs and had thought it was an alien artifact. Patricia had caught him looking at it and had stolen it back when he wasn't around. She gave it to Fabian. "Be more careful next time," she warned.

Later that day, Nina and Fabian were hanging out in Nina's room, inspecting the puzzle pieces. Nina noticed that two of the pieces had circular sections with numbers on them that turned, like a combination lock. Suddenly, she had an idea. "In my dream, Sarah was saying 'Eleven. Zero one. One nine. One five.' What if the numbers from my dream are the key to opening the puzzle pieces?" Nina paused. "The numbers sound like a date—November 1, 1915." Her eyes brightened. "I think that's Sarah's birth date!"

Nina began turning the sections. As she twisted them to reflect the last numbers of Sarah's birthday, the puzzle piece opened, revealing a hollow space. A piece of paper fluttered out. Another clue!

MY FATHER'S FATHER STANDS TALL.
HIS FACE AND HANDS TOGETHER
TURN CIRCLES AROUND ISIS AND OSIRIS,
AND HORUS, THE SON, REVEALS ME.

"I have no idea what that means," Nina said, staring at the paper. Fabian took it from her.

"Here, let me see if I can come up with something," he said.

He took the clue to his bedroom and lay down, holding it in both hands above his face. He stared at the words, his brows furrowed in concentration.

Suddenly, his eyes lit up. "My father's father is a grandfather. Isis and Osiris . . . sun and moon. Day. Night. The clock! It's the clock at the bottom of the stairs!" Fabian was elated. He ran out of his room to follow up on his new discovery. He sneaked into the hallway, crept over to the clock, and opened the glass door enclosing the face.

Fabian mused aloud, "'His face and hands together turn circles around Isis and Osiris, and Horus, the son, reveals me.'" Then the answer to the clue presented itself. "Three gods, three o'clock!" he exclaimed.

Fabian quickly moved the hands to three o'clock. He heard a soft click, and the face opened to reveal a secret compartment with the Eye of Horus painted on the rear wall. He peered in expectantly and saw . . . nothing. The compartment was empty.

Dear Diary,

Tonight I called a Sibuna meeting after Fabian told me he had solved our latest clue. When we gathered, Fabian told us he had found a secret compartment in the grandfather clock, but there was nothing in it. I told Sibuna I thought the puzzle piece I'd found in Victor's safe, the one that's identical to the latest puzzle piece we found, was originally hidden in the clock.

Fabian mentioned that since the numbers of Sarah's birth date had opened the puzzle piece we'd discovered in Victor's safe, perhaps those numbers would work on the fourth puzzle piece we had found.

I had already tried to input Sarah's birth date into the puzzle piece, with no luck. Then I had a thought. Sarah told me I'm linked to the mystery of Anubis House. What if my birth date numbers were the numbers that could open the fourth puzzle piece?

I took the unopened puzzle piece and started turning to the numbers on it to match my birth date. The house began to make strange groaning noises that grew louder with each turn.

When I turned to the last two digits of my birth

date, the puzzle piece opened, but there was no clue inside.

What happened next was really spooky. The wallpaper in my room started rippling, and then a message began to form. It read: AWAKEN THE VOICE!

What in the world does that mean?

3

Before class the next day, Nina went to the attic to clear her head. She had decided to act on a crazy whim and try to "awaken the voice" of the house by asking it for help. She took a deep breath and whispered, "Hello? House? I'm Nina. But I guess you know that. Okay, house, what do you want me to find?"

Suddenly, a wind blew through the attic. A box fell to the floor. Nina's heart jumped into her throat. "No way!" she managed to whisper.

She brought the box to her room. She opened it and found a number of old newspaper articles. Then she came across something that took her breath away. It was a clipping with a picture of Victor and Rufus shaking hands in front of a plaque. The caption read: BOARDING SCHOOL FOUNDED ON ANUBIS ESTATE.

Sarah was also in the photo. All three looked the

same age! Nina started to read the article aloud.

"'Victor Rodenmaar Junior, son of the late Victor Rodenmaar Senior, has founded a new school on the Anubis estate with help from his benefactors, Mr. Rufus Zeno and Miss Sarah Frobisher-Smythe.'"

Nina was stunned. "What was Sarah doing with Victor and Rufus all that time ago?" she thought. "And why do they all look the same age in this picture?"

Fabian entered the room just then, followed by Patricia. "What are you looking at?" he asked.

"I found this in the attic," said Nina. She gave the clipping to Fabian.

"Whoa. This photo was taken in 1960!" Fabian exclaimed. "Rufus and Victor have hardly changed since then."

"Yep. But Sarah aged normally," said Nina.

"Does this mean . . . the Elixir—" Patricia began.

"Does exist after all? Looks like it does," said Nina. "And it's not just Victor who's drinking it! Also, it looks like Victor, Sarah, and Rufus were once friends."

As Nina and Fabian pored over the clipping, Patricia heard a noise in the hallway. She peeked outside and groaned. "Guys, Alfie is coming. I had to tell him about Sibuna and the relics when he started asking questions about the puzzle piece he found."

Nina was appalled. "Alfie can't be trusted—he'll probably tell Jerome, and those two roommates always mean trouble!"

Before Patricia could apologize, Alfie bounded into the room. "Oh, wow, are we having a secret meeting?" he exclaimed. "Wicked!" He plopped down on Nina's bed.

Alfie said he wanted to confide in Nina, Fabian, and Patricia about something. He told them about a ritual involving Victor and six other men and women that he had witnessed while he was trapped in the cellar a few days before. Until now, he hadn't been able to remember anything after the event, but he was beginning to recall the details. "Mr. Sweet, Mrs. Andrews, and Mr. Winkler were there. And some other people as well. They were chanting. And they mentioned . . . the Chosen One."

Alfie took a deep breath and continued. "Then Victor drank from a skull. It was horrible. And one of them wore a mask. A dog mask." He shuddered. "I keep dreaming about that. The face . . . staring at me . . . coming for me. . . ."

Patricia squeezed his arm. "It's okay, Alfie. It's okay."

"I bet I know what they were drinking from that skull," said Nina. "The Elixir."

"What elixir?" Alfie asked.

"A potion they make. Keeps you young," Patricia replied.

Dear Diary,

The Elixir of Life is real! Today we found a photo of Sarah, Victor, and Rufus that was taken in 1960—more than fifty years ago! Even though Sarah has aged, Victor and Rufus look almost exactly the same. They must be drinking the Elixir to keep themselves young. Creepy.

Victor is scary enough, but Rufus is the one I'm really worried about. A few weeks ago, he kidnapped Patricia and tried to blackmail members of the Society to get more information about the Cup of Ankh. Amber and I found Patricia in an abandoned warehouse near the school, but Rufus locked us inside and took Patricia with him. Thank heaven for Fabian—he tracked us down and got us out of the warehouse. He was so heroic! We managed to save Patricia as well, but Rufus escaped. He is ruthless and will stop at nothing to find the Cup of Ankh before we do.

Mr. Sweet was grading essays when suddenly the door opened and Victor entered, carrying a big reference book on Egypt. He dumped it unceremoniously on Mr. Sweet's desk, sending papers flying.

"Seven!" Victor exclaimed. "The Cup of Ankh was broken into seven pieces. They must still be hidden in the house."

At that moment, the drama teacher, Jason Winkler, entered holding a newspaper.

"Mr. Sweet, have you seen the local paper's write-up of our play?" he asked. "It's rather good."

Victor frowned. "Ah, yes, the play. Mr. Winkler, did you ever find out where Nina, Fabian, and Patricia did their research for that play of yours?"

"Oh yes. They said they got the idea from some

woman at the museum. I think her name was Sarah," Jason replied.

"Well, well. Her name was Sarah, was it?" said Victor, his mind whirring. "That's very interesting!"

Victor was in the hallway. He had called the museum and found no one by the name of Sarah. He was flipping through the students' sign-out book, looking to see if there were any unusual entries. Trudy came through from the kitchen on her way to the boys' hallway with some clean linen.

"Who's this woman that Nina keeps visiting?" Victor barked.

"Just some dear lady from the old people's home that Nina has kind of adopted," replied Trudy.

Victor's ears pricked up. He was sure he had found Sarah Frobisher-Smythe. He put on his coat and left Anubis House, heading for the nursing home. Once there, he asked to see Miss Frobisher-Smythe.

"You're an old friend?" Nurse Mulligan asked Victor.

"Yes, a family friend," said Victor. "My father knew her."

Nurse Mulligan led him to Sarah, who was napping in her room. "There's a visitor here to see you," the nurse said gently.

Victor asked Nurse Mulligan to get him a cup of tea. As soon as she had left, Victor put a hand on Sarah's shoulder. "Sarah? Is that you?" he demanded.

Sarah opened her eyes. "Victor!" she gasped.

"There we go," said Nurse Mulligan to Sarah as Victor opened the front door to Anubis House. Victor had convinced the nurse that Sarah should visit her childhood home.

Sarah was frightened of Victor, but she desperately wanted to see Anubis House. As she looked into the front hallway, she started daydreaming about her childhood. She saw a vision of herself as a girl playing with her parents.

In a slightly hypnotic state, Sarah remembered having been friends with Victor many years before. But Victor's dad had threatened to send him to the orphanage if he didn't get Sarah to tell him where the Cup of Ankh was buried.

Victor, fearing his own father, had begun to abuse

Sarah. He demanded the answer from her, but she always told him she had no knowledge of the Cup of Ankh.

Sarah slowly came out of her trance and turned to Victor. "I remember now. And I understand. You only hurt me because you were afraid of your father. After my parents died, I lost you. I had no one else to talk to; I only had my diary. I counted every day I suffered without them here."

Sarah's eyes brightened and her voice grew calm. "I'm ready to go now," she said as she took a final look around the house. Nurse Mulligan led her away, and Sarah turned to Victor one last time. "I forgive you, Victor. I forgive you."

5

"*Ahhh-choo!*" Patricia sneezed violently and batted dust away from her face.

Nina, Fabian, and Patricia were in the attic, doing some sleuthing before breakfast. They were checking out the three metal cylinders they had found there. They had already listened to two of the cylinders, which were Edison phonograph recordings of Sarah's voice as a little girl, but the third appeared to be blank. In a moment of inspiration, Nina had realized the blank cylinder might be another clue and had brought her friends for a second look.

"I don't understand what we're doing here," Patricia said.

Nina held up a cylinder. "This is the cylinder that's blank. But why is it blank?"

"Because it was damaged?" Fabian suggested.

"Or . . . because it's fake," Nina replied. "This casing doesn't look right to me. Look, it's different from the others. I think it might"—she continued, pulling at the casing—"come off!" The cylinder's casing fell away.

Inside was another clue.

TO FIND THE SECRET OF THE PAST, LOOK BEYOND THIS WORLD THROUGH GLASS.

After the Sibuna members sneaked out of the attic, they headed downstairs for breakfast. While they were eating, Trudy entered and beckoned Nina outside. In the hallway, Trudy said, "There's some bad news, I'm afraid. The nursing home just called."

Nina's heart dropped. She already knew what Trudy was going to say. "Sarah's dead!"

Nina began to cry. She had lost the one person who knew the most about Anubis House. Without Sarah, how was she going to solve the mystery? What was more, Nina had lost a good friend. Trudy gave Nina a comforting hug. "Nurse Mulligan from the home wants to see you. There's something Sarah wanted you to have."

After breakfast, Nina trudged to the nursing home, feeling more awful with every step. When she arrived, Nurse Mulligan greeted her sadly. "Here," she said, handing a box to Nina. "This is for you."

As Nina took Sarah's box, Nurse Mulligan gave her a hug. "The funeral's tomorrow. You're welcome to attend."

Nina returned to Anubis House and went to her bedroom. She began sorting through the items in Sarah's box. She found a few official-looking documents, newspaper clippings, and a star chart. As she began to look at the items, there was a gentle knock at the door.

"Come in," she said.

Patricia, Fabian, and Alfie made their way into the room. "Oh, Nina—I'm so sorry," said Fabian, putting an arm around her.

"I can't believe she's gone," Nina said, wiping away a tear.

Just then, Patricia held up a piece of paper that Nina had taken from the box. It was a legal guardianship document. She read out loud. "'Gustav and Isabella Zeno'—Rufus's parents!"

"What does that mean?" asked Nina.

Fabian took the document and studied it. "It looks like Rufus's parents became Sarah's legal guardians two years after her parents died." He looked in Sarah's box, hunting for more clues. "Look! Here's a copy of Rufus's birth certificate!" His eyes widened. "He was born in 1915—he's the same age as Sarah!"

6

It was the day of Sarah's funeral. A cold, bitter breeze blew across the cloudy sky. Nina gently placed a rose on Sarah's casket. "Goodbye, Sarah," she whispered. In the distance, a raven cawed.

Afterward, Nina returned to the nursing home to see if Sarah had left her any more clues besides the box. As she approached Sarah's room, she heard two men talking. She pressed against the wall and took a quick peek into the room. Victor and Rufus were there! She shrank back and listened.

"What exactly are you looking for, Zeno?" Victor said.

"Victor. How lovely to see you," Rufus replied calmly.

"I wish I could say the same," retorted Victor. "You have something that belongs to me."

"The Elixir of Life?" Rufus laughed. "All gone. Or very nearly. Same as your supply, I'd imagine."

"I'm not talking about your theft from years ago. I mean the things you took from my safe," said Victor.

Nina stifled a cry. Rufus hadn't taken the puzzle pieces from Victor's safe—*she* had! But instead of denying the theft, Rufus asked Victor what he would give in return for the puzzle pieces.

"I don't do deals," Victor told Rufus.

"Come, come." Nina could hear the sneer in Rufus's voice. "You know that's not true. We did a deal all those years ago to swindle Sarah out of her home."

"Sarah wanted to sell. She always hated the place," replied Victor.

"Well, that's in the past. Now it's time to think about the future." There was a pause. "Where is the Chosen One?" said Rufus.

"Where are the Ankh pieces?" Victor demanded.

"We're going round in circles, old man. You do realize that Joy by herself is totally useless," Rufus replied.

"If you mean do I also have the seven acolytes, then yes, it has all been arranged," Victor said.

Rufus laughed. "Oh yes, the tipping of the Scales of Life. That old legend. Now, you had better tell me where Joy is or I will make you. Because only I know what will really happen when the Cup and the Chosen One come together."

At that moment, Nurse Mulligan ran past Nina and burst into the room. She gasped. "What have you done?" she said to the two men. Nina looked inside. Sarah's room was a wreck. Drawers and closets had been ransacked, and the bed had been flipped over.

Both Victor and Rufus turned to see Nina standing in the doorway.

Rufus darted past Victor and rushed out. Victor locked eyes with Nina. She could see the anger and alarm in them. Without a word, he stalked past her and headed back to Anubis House.

Nina waited until she was sure she wouldn't run into Victor. Then she raced to Anubis House and called an emergency Sibuna meeting in the dining room. Fabian, Amber, Patricia, and Alfie gathered around the table.

"Rufus said that Joy was the 'Chosen One' during his argument with Victor," Nina said.

"I told you she was part of it," Alfie said.

Patricia bristled. "She is not part of it, Alfie! Joy would never betray us." She sighed. "I've got to get ahold of her!"

Nina continued. "Rufus used to be in a Society with Victor, but Victor threw him out. And Victor thinks Rufus has the puzzle pieces," she explained. "But he called them Ankh pieces." She looked around. "I think the puzzle pieces are more than just clues!"

Fabian also had news. Earlier in the day he had heard Mr. Sweet talk about initiating Jason Winkler into the Society that night. The ceremony would be held in the cellar.

"So we're going back down to the cellar?" Alfie asked. Fabian nodded grimly.

That night, Fabian and Alfie were already in the kitchen when Nina, Amber, and Patricia joined them. Amber was lugging a heavy backpack. "What's in the bag?" Fabian asked.

Amber swung the bag over her shoulder. "Supplies, in case of an emergency."

"We won't need supplies," groaned Fabian, but he let Amber keep her bag.

As the students prepared to descend into the cellar, Patricia held back. "I'm staying up here," she said. "There's something I have to do."

Nina smiled knowingly and gave a salute. "Good luck getting in touch with Joy," she said.

Patricia saluted back and disappeared down the hallway.

Nina led the rest of the group into the cellar using the secret entrance in the kitchen. Once they reached the bottom of the secret passageway, they found a hiding place and settled down to wait.

It was freezing and damp in the cellar. Amber noticed Fabian shivering and pulled a warm coat out of her bag. "Does anyone else want anything?" she asked innocently.

"Actually, yeah," said Fabian reluctantly.

"See—the bag's not such a bad idea now, is it?" Amber said triumphantly. She pulled out a dark-colored blanket and handed it to Fabian, then pulled out a red blanket for Nina. "Here you go, Nina," she said.

Nina shook her head, waving it away. "It's too bright, Amber. It might be seen."

"You can, er—you can share this if you want," Fabian offered. He held his blanket out. Nina scooted next to him, grateful that the cellar was dark so no one could see her blush.

All four Sibuna members sat in silence, huddled together in their hiding spot.

7

It was dark outside when the hidden students heard the front door of Anubis House open. Six Society members entered and greeted Victor, who led them down into the cellar, right past the students.

The Sibuna members immediately recognized Jason Winkler; Mr. Sweet; Mrs. Andrews; Joy's dad, Frederick Mercer; and the school nurse, Nurse Delia. Patricia silently pointed out Sergeant Roebuck, who had deceived her about Joy's disappearance several weeks before.

The Sibuna members sat stock-still as Victor started lighting candles at an altar while the teachers and the others put on ceremonial robes.

"It's time for you to become a full member of the Society, Jason," Victor announced.

"You already know about the Elixir of Life," said Mrs. Andrews.

Jason nodded. "Brewed by Victor's father. Slows down the aging process."

"I am walking proof. How old do you think I am, Jason?" Victor asked.

Jason shook his head. Victor smiled. "Ninety-five years of age. Ninety-five!"

Victor went to the cupboard and took out a small vial of golden liquid. The Sibuna members saw this and looked at each other wide-eyed. Now they knew where the Elixir of Life was kept.

"Oh yes. It's a potent beverage. Unfortunately, this is all we have left," Victor said, showing the vial to Jason.

Mrs. Andrews explained that Victor's father had died in an accident before he could pass on the secret of the Elixir. Mr. Sweet added that Victor had tried many times over many years to replicate his father's recipe, but had been unsuccessful.

Victor held up his hand. "None of that will matter soon. Once we put the Cup of Ankh and the Chosen One together, we won't need the Elixir anymore.

We can tip the Scales of Life and all become truly immortal."

Frederick Mercer spoke up. "Legend has it that when a person drinks the Elixir of Life from the Cup of Ankh, that person attains immortality."

"And one day very soon we will achieve it," Victor continued. He began an incantation.

"*Yo dee en en en ankh. Yo dee en en ra nekekh.* We pledge ourselves to Ankh. To eternity."

The teachers and the others repeated the incantation.

"*Yo dee en en en ankh. Yo dee en en ra nekekh.* We pledge ourselves to Ankh. To eternity."

Victor placed the Anubis mask on Jason and moved him into the middle of a circle. The others walked around him, chanting.

Victor walked to a table and began boiling up a concoction. A large box lay to the right of him. As the rest of the Society members circled Jason, Victor poured the Elixir into a skull. He took a snake from the box and held it in Jason's direction. "We welcome you, novice, and deliver you from the valley of the dead to the mountain of eternal life."

Victor held the snake over the skull and squeezed

venom into it. He began to drink from the skull while the others continued to repeat the incantation.

"*Yo dee en en en ankh. Yo dee en en ra nekekh.* We pledge ourselves to the Ankh. To eternity."

Upstairs, Patricia was searching Victor's office for a number to call Joy. Patricia noticed Corbiere's dead eyes staring at her. "What are you looking at?" she asked the stuffed bird. As she turned it around, she saw a piece of paper beneath its claw. She read it and realized it was Frederick Mercer's video call address. She pulled up the video call site on the computer and dialed the address, keeping one eye on the screen and the other on the door. Suddenly, Joy appeared on the screen, looking like she had just woken up.

"Hello? Patricia, is that you?" she asked sleepily.

Patricia gasped. "Joy! Listen—I don't have much time. What do you know about the secret Society that Victor's in?" she asked.

Joy hesitated. "My dad . . . has been conned into some weird organization run by Victor and the teachers. I don't know much about it except they've told my dad that because I was born at seven o'clock on the seventh day of the seventh month, I'm the Chosen One. But what does it all mean?" Joy's face crumpled. "I don't want to be the Chosen One. I want to watch TV and hang out with you and take physics tests. I want to be normal."

Patricia looked at her best friend on Victor's screen. "We'll sort this out. But we need to keep in touch. Can you get ahold of a cell phone?"

"I'm not sure," Joy said.

"Please try," begged Patricia. "And text me with your new number soon, okay?" She heard a noise in the hallway and quickly shut off Victor's computer, then ducked down. When she raised her head, there was no one in the hallway. She carefully put the video call address back under Corbiere's feet and dashed to a hiding place in the kitchen to wait for the other Sibuna members.

Late that night, the Sibuna members emerged from the cellar. Patricia came out of her hiding spot and they exchanged information about what they had found. Nina told Patricia about the Cup of Ankh, and Patricia told the Sibuna members about getting in touch with Joy.

"Victor must really want to stay young. He actually drank snake poison! I mean, why doesn't he just have plastic surgery?" Amber said.

Nina said it wasn't safe to talk in the kitchen, so the students headed back to their rooms. None of them noticed a figure peeking out from the next room. When the Sibuna members were gone, the figure stepped out of the shadows. He had a big smile on his face.

"Very interesting. Let the fun begin," Jerome said to himself.

8

The next day during their lunch break, the Sibuna members gathered next to the bike shed. Nina opened her bag and laid out all of the puzzle pieces in front of them.

Nina began. "Okay, after seeing what we saw last night, our top priority is the Cup of Ankh. We have to find it before they do!" Nina picked up a puzzle piece. "These objects are the key somehow. But until we've got them all, we won't know exactly what that key is." She paused. "Knowing Victor, I don't think it's safe to keep the puzzle pieces in our rooms. After school I'm going to hide them in the secret room in the attic."

Patricia looked at her watch. "Guys, we have to go. Lunch is almost over—we'll be late for class."

Nina gathered up the puzzle pieces, and the

Sibuna members headed back to school.

"I've suspected for a long time that someone has been coming up to the attic," Victor said to Nina. "What's in here that's so very interesting, Miss Martin?"

Nina had just hidden the puzzle pieces in the attic, and she'd been caught red-handed trying to lock the door with her bobby pin. Victor had forced her back into the attic and begun searching it for clues. He had found the Edison phonograph and was examining it.

"This is an antique. It could be valuable. Have you been tampering with it?"

Nina shook her head, her eyes darting back and forth. Victor was standing near the hidden room. He ran his fingers across the secret panel.

"Why did you come up to the attic?" he shouted.

Nina thought quickly. "I've always lived on my own, just me and Gran. It was always very quiet. Sometimes I need to get away to think," she replied.

"Well, not anymore. There's a padlock going on that door, so you can forget about any more 'me time' in the attic. Now go!" commanded Victor.

Nina made a quick exit. Victor took one last look around. He picked up the Edison phonograph and took it downstairs.

Fabian, Patricia, and Jerome were lounging in the living room. Patricia had just gotten a text from Joy, who had found a phone. As Fabian and Patricia celebrated, Nina rushed in. She told them that Victor had caught her. Noticing Jerome, she frowned. She didn't want him listening in on a Sibuna conversation, so she beckoned for Fabian and Patricia to join her in the hallway. In a hushed voice, Nina told them the puzzle pieces were safe in the attic, but Victor was going to put a padlock on the attic door.

"How will we get the puzzle pieces out if he does that?" Fabian asked.

The group stared glumly at one another.

Back in the living room, Jerome was about to spy on Nina, Fabian, and Patricia when his eyes lighted on Patricia's cell phone. Patricia had left it on the coffee table. Jerome picked up the phone and looked at the most recent calls. He noticed that the number for an "RZ" had been dialed several of times. He didn't know that RZ stood for "Rufus Zeno," the man who had befriended Patricia and then kidnapped her to try to get information about the Cup of Ankh.

Jerome quickly typed the number into his phone and put Patricia's phone back on the coffee table just before the gang trooped back into the room.

Jerome immediately dialed the number.

"Hello. My name's Jerome Clarke—I live in Anubis House." There was a pause as Jerome listened. "I think you'd be very interested in meeting me," he said with a grin.

Moonlight streamed through the wooden slats of the bike shed, casting an eerie glow. Inside, Jerome nervously stood waiting to meet Rufus.

Suddenly, Rufus stepped out of the shadows. "Jerome Clarke?" he asked.

Jerome nodded. After they had shaken hands, Jerome began. "So . . . about the treasure."

Rufus grabbed Jerome's arm. "You have the Cup of Ankh? Where is it? Tell me," he snarled.

Jerome drew back in fear. "Ow! Get off! I haven't found anything."

Rufus regained his composure. "I'm sorry, but the Cup of Ankh is very important to me."

Jerome smiled slyly. "Is it worth a lot of money?"

Rufus glared at him. "It's priceless. Tell me what you know!"

Jerome took a deep breath. "Okay. But it'll cost you."

Rufus looked sternly at Jerome, who began to sweat. Rufus smiled and pulled out a twenty-pound note. He handed it to Jerome. "There's plenty more where that came from if you have the right information. Now spill."

Jerome didn't know much about the activities of Sibuna, but he told Rufus about the secret ritual in the basement that had been witnessed by Nina, Fabian, Alfie, and Amber.

"Nina Martin?" Rufus said.

"Yes," Jerome said.

Under his breath, Rufus muttered, "The girl with the locket."

Jerome continued, telling Rufus that the gang seemed pretty close to finding the treasure, which was some kind of cup. Rufus looked ecstatic at the news and again muttered to himself. "So, it was in the house after all." He took out his wallet and peeled off a wad of twenty-pound notes. He handed them to Jerome.

"Here," he said. "Consider this a down payment. I want to know everything."

"No problem," Jerome replied eagerly.

"Good lad," said Rufus with a satisfied smile.

9

"Why is it always one step forward, five steps back, Fabian?" Nina said with a sigh as she gazed out her bedroom window. She was looking at the last clue and repeating it out loud. "'To find the secret of the past, look beyond this world through glass.'"

Fabian shrugged, put down his guitar, and joined her at the window. As he stared at the star-filled night, a thought suddenly struck him.

"'Beyond this world through glass,'" he said slowly. "The stars. Beyond the world." He turned to Nina. "How do people normally look at the stars?"

"Through a telescope!" Nina exclaimed. "There's one in the living room. Let's go!"

They rushed to the living room, and sure enough, there was the dusty telescope in one of the corners. Fabian set it up by the window.

"What am I looking for? I can't see anything," Nina complained as she looked through the old telescope lens.

"'Look beyond this world. . . .' To the moon, perhaps? Try focusing on the moon," Fabian replied.

As Nina focused on the moon, its brightness revealed small, dark letters etched on the glass of the telescope. "There's something here!" She pulled Fabian in front of the telescope. "Take a look. What does it say?"

"'Unleash the power and light your way. Find the demisphere hidden below,'" Fabian read aloud. He looked at Nina with a wide grin. "Yes!" he said. "We're back in business. Sibuna!"

Dear Diary,

Another close call with Victor! Fabian and I had just discovered another clue etched onto the lens of the telescope in the living room when Victor spotted us. "Doing a little stargazing, are we?" he said, and came over to the telescope. Fabian and I froze. Victor was about to see the next clue!

Victor bent and looked through the eyepiece, then straightened. "Only you, Fabian, would choose such a cloudy night to stargaze," he said. In the nick of time, a cloud had covered the moon and the clue had disappeared!

Victor told us to get to our rooms, and Fabian and I fled, so relieved. Fabian made sure I was okay, then headed to his room. It took a long time for my heart to stop pounding.

10

"The riddle definitely said 'Light your way. Find the demisphere hidden below,'" Nina told the Sibuna members at breakfast the next morning.

"But what's a demisphere?" asked Alfie. Nobody knew.

Patricia spoke up. "Perhaps 'hidden below' means the next clue is in the cellar."

Amber shuddered. "I really do *not* want to go back into that creepy old cellar."

Fabian tapped his chin thoughtfully. "Clue or not, we still need to go back down to get a sample of the Elixir." He looked at Amber's horrified face. "Maybe this time only one of us will have to go, and the others can keep watch."

"Yes! Great plan, Fabs. I'll stay here and hold down the fort." Amber breathed a sigh of relief.

"Shall we draw straws for it?" Fabian asked.

Amber wrinkled her eyebrows. "Or we can do it that way," she said dejectedly.

Patricia, Nina, and Fabian got to class early, and Nina cut up some straws. Alfie and Jerome arrived at the same time a few minutes later. Jerome was holding a wad of twenty-pound notes and counting them.

"Whoa, man, have you won the lottery?" Alfie asked.

"Something like that, Alfie. Now get over there and check out what the gang is up to and you might get that magic set you have been wanting for so long," Jerome replied.

Alfie wandered over to where Nina, Patricia, and Fabian were standing. Nina asked him what he and Jerome had been talking about.

"Oh, you know. The usual. Where to hang. What to scam. Who to snarl at. I'm fed up with him, to be honest," Alfie said, looking slightly uncomfortable.

The gang gathered together to draw the straws Nina had cut. Alfie drew the shortest straw. Nina said she wasn't sure Alfie was ready for the task.

"Why not? You still don't trust me, do you?" Alfie said. "Let me prove I can be a true Sibuna. Anyway, I was fine last time I was down there."

"Okay, okay. Alfie it is," sighed Nina.

That night, Amber, Patricia, Nina, and Fabian waited for Alfie in the kitchen, by the entrance to the secret passage. Alfie arrived wearing full combat gear, a Rambo-style bandana, and camouflage makeup, his backpack slung across his shoulders.

"What are you dressed up for?" Fabian asked.

"Take no notice. I think you look very nice, Alfie," Amber said.

Nina asked him if he knew what he was doing. "Getting a sample of the Elixir and looking for a demisphere—whatever a demisphere is," Alfie responded.

Nina nodded. She opened the secret passage with her locket. "Good luck," she said. Alfie moved toward the passage, suddenly looking nervous about going into the cellar alone.

"Amber?" he said.

"Yeah?"

"Can I have a good-luck kiss?"

"Aww! Course you can, Boo," Amber replied, giving him a big smack on his cheek.

"Thanks. I can face anything now," Alfie said with a big smile.

Alfie disappeared into the passage. Once he was in the cellar, he took the vial of Elixir from the secret cupboard and put it in his backpack. Then he shone his flashlight around, looking for anything that might be the demisphere.

11

When Alfie got to breakfast, the other Sibuna members gave him a little cheer. "How did you do last night?" Patricia asked him. "Did you find anything?"

Alfie pulled out the vial of Elixir and handed it to Fabian. He received more cheers and some pats on the back. "Good work, Alfie," said Nina.

Amber told Alfie they had decided to make him an official member of the Sibuna club. "You did a really brave thing, going into the cellar. And you got the Elixir! You are one of us now," she said.

"I'm sorry I ever doubted your loyalty," Patricia added.

"When you were in the cellar, did you find the demisphere?" Fabian asked.

Alfie shook his head. "I looked everywhere, but I couldn't see anything that looked right."

Jerome arrived at the table, and the Sibuna members quickly turned the conversation to other subjects. After breakfast, Alfie went to his room to hang out with Jerome.

"So what were you all up to last night, then?" Jerome asked Alfie casually. "Looking for the Cup of Ankh?"

"How do you know about the Cup—" Alfie began, before realizing he had given away too much.

"Gotcha!" said Jerome triumphantly. "I know plenty, Alfie. But I need to know more. There's someone paying me big bucks for information on all this. I can cut you in on it if you'd like; you just need to help me out a bit." Jerome grinned deviously. "So come on, tell me what you know."

Jerome was carrying a load of shopping bags to his room when his phone rang. It was Rufus, who told Jerome he had been waiting to hear from him. Jerome had nothing to report yet, but he now had someone on the inside working for him.

"Make sure you get me what I have paid for. By tomorrow. Noon. Same place," Rufus ordered.

Jerome hung up and decided he had to use Alfie to make Rufus happy. During lunch, he made a quick stop at a sports store, then headed to Anubis House to wait.

When Alfie came into the room, Jerome was lying on his bed reading a magazine. Alfie found a new hat on his bed, and Jerome told him he had felt like treating his friend.

As soon as Alfie put the hat on, Jerome began to guilt-trip him. "Alfie, friends tell each other everything. If you want to remain my friend, you have to tell me everything you know about Nina and her little friends."

Alfie didn't want to betray Sibuna, but Jerome kept bullying him until he broke. "They've got this Elixir stuff," Alfie said, "and if you drink it out of the Cup of Ankh, it keeps you young."

Jerome asked Alfie if he had any Elixir. Alfie said Fabian had it, so Jerome ordered him to steal it. Alfie said no, but Jerome knew exactly how to pressure him. "Steal it for me and you'll prove you're my friend," he said.

12

Before dinner that evening, Nina stood in the hallway, deep in thought. Her eyes were drawn up toward the chandelier. The circle of lights emitted a strange glow for a second.

"What is so fascinating up there, Miss Martin?" Victor said as he came down the stairs, making Nina jump. She hurried past him to her room. When she left, Victor looked up suspiciously but couldn't see anything. He went and got a stepladder to climb up and take a closer look.

Nina went into her bedroom. She opened her locket and looked at the picture of Sarah. Amber entered and told her she had nearly knocked Victor off his stepladder while he was changing a lightbulb in the hall. Nina jumped to her feet and rushed to the door. "What's wrong?" Amber asked.

"I think the next clue is hidden in there. We have to stop Victor. Now! Help me!" Nina shouted back as she rushed from the room.

Victor was examining the chandelier when the two girls arrived at the top of the stairs. Amber sprang into action. "Victor, I don't feel very well . . . ," she said, before falling into an elaborate faint. Nina caught her before she hit the floor.

"Victor, quick! Amber's fainted!" Nina shouted.

Victor got down from the stepladder. When he reached the top of the stairs, Amber started moaning. Victor helped her to her feet and told Nina to go and get Trudy. He helped Amber to her room, and Nina climbed up to the chandelier and examined it. At the bottom of the chandelier was a globe.

Nina turned the sphere and it came apart. The bottom half fell into her hand. "The demisphere!" Nina whispered excitedly. She looked inside. A piece of parchment fell out and fluttered to the floor.

Nina reached into the demisphere and pulled out another puzzle piece, which was shaped like a teardrop. Just then, she heard Victor calling her name. She quickly put the puzzle piece in her pocket, fastened the demisphere back into place, and climbed down the ladder. Victor arrived just as Nina was putting her foot over the next clue.

"What are you doing? Where's Trudy?" he asked.

Amber had crept to the top of the stairs. "Victor!" she shouted. "The room's starting to spin. And I think my ankles are swelling up! I'm going to faint again."

Victor glanced up at Amber. At that moment, Nina knelt down and quickly grabbed the clue.

"Trudy will be with you presently," said Victor.

Nina took her cue. "Yes—Trudy! I'll go get her." She dashed to the kitchen, where Trudy was washing dishes.

"Trudy, Amber's fainted!" yelled Nina. Trudy wiped her hands and darted up the stairs.

Nina unfolded the next clue and Fabian entered the room. He looked at the parchment. "Wow! Where was it?" he said.

"In the demisphere, which was at the bottom of the chandelier," said Nina.

She smoothed out the piece of parchment.

INSIDE THE CORE OF MY ENEMY'S PRIDE IS WHERE THE FINAL RELIC HIDES.

The closer Nina gets to the truth about the
Cup of Ankh, the more danger she encounters.

Fabian wants to protect Nina from the perils
of Anubis House—but what will it cost him?

Amber may be slightly ditzy, but she knows
exactly what to do to keep the Sibuna club together.

Jerome is the king of schemes—until
he tries to con the wrong guy.

After a rocky start, Alfie proves
his worth as a Sibuna member.

Is Joy truly The Chosen One—or has there been a huge mix-up?

How far will Victor Rodenmaar go to
protect the dark secrets of Anubis House?

Can Nina and the Sibuna club find
the Cup of Ankh before time runs out?

They looked at each other.

"Final relic?" said Fabian.

Nina grinned. "Yes!"

Fabian looked at Nina thoughtfully. "I'm wondering if . . . if they've got it wrong about Joy being the Chosen One," he said hesitantly. "I'm beginning to believe that it's you, Nina!"

While Nina and Fabian were thinking about the last clue, Alfie and Jerome lounged in their room. They had hatched a plan to steal the Elixir from under Fabian's bed on laundry day so that they could lay the blame on Trudy. Jerome clenched his fingers. "I've got to get that Elixir."

"I have something that might help until we get it," Alfie said suddenly. "There are these puzzles pieces. They're like . . . clues that lead to the treasure. Nina just found another one today. I can draw them. Then if you show it to the fellow who wants it, he'll realize you know what you're talking about."

Jerome scoffed. "Drawings! I hardly think drawings will be enough!"

"You never know," Alfie replied, and sat down at his

desk to draw while Jerome sat on his bed and sulked.

At supper, Jerome wolfed down his meal and abruptly left the dining room without a word to anyone.

"That's odd," thought Alfie. "Jerome normally hangs around to bother everyone for a while." He ran down the corridor. The door to Fabian's room was ajar, so he pushed it open the rest of the way and found Jerome looking around Fabian's bed.

"What are you doing? We agreed we'd wait a few days before taking the Elixir!" Alfie cried.

"*You* agreed, not me." Jerome looked around in disgust. "Anyway, it's not here."

"What?" said Alfie.

"The Elixir isn't here. Your new buddies are feeding you false information, Alfie. They obviously don't trust you," sneered Jerome.

Alfie was hurt. He didn't know who or what to believe anymore.

Jerome saw his chance to take advantage of Alfie. "Come on, mate," he said. "Let's have a look at these scribble drawings of yours." Alfie reluctantly handed over his drawings of the Ankh pieces. Jerome studied them. "Well, they're not great, but I have a meeting with Rufus tonight. Maybe these drawings will do."

"Rufus!" Alfie snatched the drawings back. "You didn't tell me you were working with Rufus! He's a madman!" he shouted, and ran out of the room with Jerome hot on his heels.

Alfie dashed down the hallway, burst into the kitchen—and ran straight into Victor. Jerome, who was right behind him, came to a halt and quickly backed out of the kitchen.

Victor looked down at the drawings, and his face turned pale. He took them out of Alfie's hands, turned around, and walked out of the kitchen. He headed up the stairs and into his office, locking the door behind him. With nervous fingers, he began dialing all the members of the Society. He gave each of them the same message: somehow the Anubis House students had the Ankh pieces.

After failing to get any of the Ankh pieces, or even Alfie's drawings, Jerome headed to the bike shed, where he had to planned to meet Rufus. When Jerome arrived, Rufus was waiting impatiently. "What have you got for me?" he said.

"I've found out loads of stuff," Jerome babbled. "They've got a bottle of that Elixir hidden somewhere, and they've also got these weird objects, which are like clues to the treasure, and . . ."

"But what have you got for me?" asked Rufus. His voice was dangerously low.

"Er . . . I've actually got . . . nothing," said Jerome.

Rufus suddenly pushed Jerome against a wall. "You have twenty-four hours to get me something concrete; otherwise I will mummify you alive. And that is not just a figure of speech. Trust me."

"I'll get something for you, I promise!" Jerome yelped, terrified.

"Make sure you do," said Rufus. He let go of Jerome and walked away.

"Was it just me, or was Alfie acting really strange?" asked Nina. It was after dinner, and she and Fabian were in her room talking about the latest developments.

"He really was. I'm glad we moved the Elixir," Fabian replied.

Patricia came in holding the newest clue. "Come on, guys, we need your help to solve this puzzle. Amber and I are getting nowhere."

Nina took the clue and read it again. "'Inside the core of my enemy's pride is where the final relic hides.'"

Amber walked in. "Core, core, what is the core?"

Patricia jumped up. "Caw, caw. You sound just like Corbiere!"

Nina thought for a moment. "Victor's father became the enemy of the Frobisher-Smythe family. And Corbiere was his pride and joy."

"So the final clue is inside Corbiere?" asked Patricia.

Nina nodded. "I think so, yes. Sarah's dad must have known it would be the last place anyone would look."

"In a stuffed bird right under their noses. The guy had a sense of humor," said Fabian.

"We'll have to sneak into Victor's office and take a look inside Corbiere," said Nina.

Amber groaned. "I just wish that one time we could go somewhere we are allowed!"

Nina stood up. "Fabian and I can take care of

this together." She turned to Fabian. "Let's go see if Victor is out of his office."

Nina and Fabian ran down the hallway, just in time to see Victor head down the stairs and out the front door. "This is our chance!" Fabian said. They dashed into Victor's office. Nina picked up Corbiere and looked for a secret compartment.

"A simple twist of Corbiere's head should work," said Fabian.

Nina made a sound of disgust. Fabian shrugged apologetically. "I saw it in a movie once."

"What kinds of movies do you like to watch?" Nina asked, laughing. She gingerly twisted Corbiere's head, and it came off in her hand. "Gross!"

Fabian put his hand inside Corbiere and pulled out a small broochlike puzzle piece on which were engraved three letters: E N D.

"What does that mean?" Nina said.

"Maybe it means we've come to the end of the search?" said Fabian.

Nina furrowed her eyebrows. "We now have seven puzzle pieces, but where's the Cup of Ankh?"

13

Nina blinked her eyes open, squinting at the bright morning sun flooding through her bedroom window. She yawned and padded to the bathroom, where Patricia and Amber were brushing their teeth. As she combed her hair, Nina told the girls about the newest clue.

"But how can it mean the end of the search? We haven't found the Cup of Ankh yet," said Patricia, toothpaste spraying from her mouth.

"It could mean the end of the clues," said Nina. "And if there are no more clues, we must examine all the pieces again. The answers are there, I just know it."

"Let's hope it doesn't lead to more creepy stuffed animals," said Amber as she pulled back the curtain, took off her bathrobe, and jumped into the shower. Suddenly, there was a bloodcurdling scream from downstairs. At the same time, Amber leapt out of the shower with a yell. "Mice!" she screeched, then threw on her bathrobe and tore out of the bathroom.

By lunchtime, Mrs. Andrews had announced that a pest controller had been called. Anubis House was infested with white mice, and all the students were to spend the night in the main school building. "Think of it as a little adventure," said Mrs. Andrews as she ushered the students out of the house. "Now, you all know the rules about food in dormitories. We'll be searching your rooms for snacks, just as a precaution against the mice."

Nina was collecting a few personal items when Alfie ran up to her. He told her that Victor had discovered the drawings he had made of the Ankh pieces.

"Victor knows we have the Ankh pieces! He's going to search the place and find everything for sure," whispered Nina, horrified.

That evening, Trudy handed out inflatable mattresses and sleeping bags to the Anubis House students staying at the school. Fabian and Nina collected take-out food orders from the students. Nina tried to act normal, but she was shaking with fear. After they had finished, Fabian drew Nina aside and tried to reassure her. "Most of the puzzle pieces and the recordings are safe in the attic. And you've got the last two pieces in your bag. Victor isn't going to find them."

"We've got to get back to the house and get the other pieces!" Nina exclaimed. "Knowing Victor, he'll tear apart everything to find them!"

Trudy bounded over. "Isn't this exciting? It's like a camping trip. Now, the boys will be in the classroom." She pointed to the left. "Girls through there in the common room. Nina, have you got all the take-out orders?"

"Yes. I'll need to go outside to use my cell phone to place the order," Nina said. "No reception in here." She hoped Trudy would let her out so she could race back to the house and grab the other puzzle pieces.

"There's no need for that," said Mr. Sweet. "You can use the phone in my office."

Nina thanked Mr. Sweet through gritted teeth. He led her to his office, where she placed the order.

As she hung up the phone, Mr. Sweet stretched. "Looks like I'm here for the night taking care of you students," he said, settling down to do some paperwork.

As she headed out, Nina got an idea. While Mr. Sweet wasn't looking, she stole his office key. She rushed back to the Sibuna members and told them her plan. Once they had all heard it, Nina sprang into action.

She found their house mom in the lounge. "Trudy, we were just saying, we never ordered any food for poor Mr. Sweet. We thought maybe you could take a menu to his office."

"That's so thoughtful of you. I'll go find him now," said Trudy, grabbing the menu. As she disappeared down the hallway, she called, "Be good, everybody; I won't be long."

As soon as she had left, Nina asked Patricia to act as a lookout before following Trudy to Mr. Sweet's office. While Mr. Sweet deliberated over his order, Nina drew out the office key and quietly closed and locked his door. She grabbed Fabian and they sneaked out of the school and ran toward the house.

When Trudy tried to leave Mr. Sweet's office, she

couldn't open the door. Mr. Sweet moved her aside and tried, but he couldn't open it either. "Whatever could have happened here?" he said, irritated. "No matter, I will call Victor. He has a master key."

Jerome watched as Nina and Fabian fled into the night. Determined to discover where they were going, he went to find Alfie, who was enjoying a sack race with Amber. "What are your little friends up to, Alfie?" Jerome demanded.

Alfie hopped over to Jerome. Jerome pointed a finger toward the door. "Follow them. Find out what they're up to," he ordered.

"I'm not your lapdog, you know," Alfie replied.

Jerome scowled. "Oh yes, you are. If I say jump, you jump, and then roll over."

"No," said Alfie firmly. "I thought you were my friend. I was wrong. You have never been my friend. You have never been anyone's friend." He turned away and went back to Amber, leaving Jerome alone.

14

"Finally, Corbiere, we have the house completely to ourselves. Let the search begin," said Victor as he stood in Fabian's room. After he had informed the Society that the Anubis House students had the Ankh pieces, Victor had devised a desperate plan. He had gone to the pet store, bought a cage full of mice, and released them into the house. With the Anubis House students gone, he could search for the Ankh pieces at his leisure.

Victor nearly demolished Fabian's room before he found a notebook filled with the solutions of various clues and puzzles. He popped it into his bag triumphantly.

He then left the boys' room and headed to Nina and Amber's room. He turned the place upside down but found nothing. In his desperation, he even decapitated some teddy bears and flung them to the floor. Finally, he pulled the mattress off Nina's bed. His eyes widened. The Elixir was there! Victor opened the vial and sniffed it to check its authenticity. "How did they . . . how could they . . . ?" he said aloud. He shook his head in disbelief, put the vial in his bag, and continued searching.

His next stop was the attic.

Victor found the secret room by pure luck. After searching fruitlessly for clues, he grew violent. Furious at his lack of progress, he threw a bat at the false wall, cracking the plaster. Then he picked up the bat and smashed it repeatedly into the wall.

The phone started to ring downstairs. "Go away, whoever you are," cried Victor, in no mood to answer it. Eventually, the ringing stopped, and Victor ripped through the false wall. Just then, the phone began to ring again.

"Oh, all right, I'm coming," he snarled, and hurried down to his office. He picked up the phone. "Yes, all right!" he said furiously when he'd heard of Mr. Sweet and Trudy's predicament. "I'm on my way over now."

15

Fabian and Nina were crouched behind some bushes, watching the front of the house. "So if everything goes according to plan, as soon as Trudy and Mr. Sweet realize they're locked in, they'll call Victor, and he'll go over to let them out. That's when we make our move," Nina said.

"Why is it taking so long, though? They must have realized by now!" Fabian said.

"Don't worry, they'll call him. Victor's the only person with a master key. He's made sure of that," Nina said, just as Victor strode out of the house.

"Okay, we've got about ten minutes max. Let's go," said Fabian. The two raced inside and went up to Nina's room. Nina gasped at the disaster. She rushed to her bed.

"Fabian, the Elixir's gone!" she cried.

Fabian groaned.

Nina tugged at Fabian's elbow. "Quick, let's go and check on the puzzle pieces."

Nina and Fabian each gave a huge sigh of relief when they reached the attic. The wall had been torn open, but Victor hadn't yet discovered the puzzle pieces. Nina quickly put them in her bag.

"Okay, we need to go, or they're going to know we're missing," said Fabian.

As they hurried down the attic steps, the cylinder recordings lay forgotten in plain sight.

Victor opened Mr. Sweet's door. "I smell a rat," he said grimly, marching down the corridor, followed by Mr. Sweet and Trudy. Patricia, watching from the girls' common room, knew she had to stall them. She slipped into the corridor and barred their way.

"Sorry. You can't go in just yet," she said.

"Why not?" said Victor angrily.

Patricia thought quickly. "The girls are getting changed for bed."

Victor asked her where the boys were. "Gone . . . to the bathroom. You know how boys are . . . always going to the bathroom in groups . . . ," Patricia said feebly. Victor sent Trudy to check on the girls while he went to the boys' bathroom.

Victor was beside himself when he discovered that Nina and Fabian were missing. "Where are they?" he yelled. "They've gone to the house, haven't they?" Patricia had run out of stalling tactics. Not waiting for an answer, Victor raced down the hallway, shouting, "We've been tricked!"

Just then, Nina and Fabian sauntered around the corner carrying pizza boxes and Chinese take-out containers. "Where have you two been?" demanded Victor. "You were given strict orders not to leave the common room."

"I got a phone call from the deliveryman. He was outside the main doors, so we went to get our food," Nina replied in a nonchalant tone.

Victor wasn't convinced, but he was more concerned about Anubis House. He darted back to see if things were as he had left them.

Nina and Fabian looked at each other and smirked. "How lucky was that—bumping into the delivery guy on the way over?" said Nina, suppressing a laugh.

When Victor returned to the attic, he found the cylinders and Sarah's portrait lying in the secret room. "Sarah, Sarah. Why did you have to go and die on me just when I'd found you again?" Victor lamented, picking up the painting. As he leaned the portrait against the wall, he noticed some hieroglyphics on the back. "What's this?" he said to himself. "Hmm, very interesting."

Dear Diary,

Victor came so close to discovering the puzzle pieces! After we were let back into Anubis House, I called a Sibuna meeting. We decided to divide the seven puzzle pieces up for safekeeping. Fabian took two, I took two, Amber took one—the prettiest—and Patricia and Alfie took one each. I told everyone we must swear to carry the pieces with us at all times and guard them with our lives. Everyone said, "Sibuna!" and went to hide their pieces in their bags.

Joy had told us to trust Victor, but after what he did to our rooms, I really don't think he's on our side. And speaking of people not to trust, I worry about Jerome. He's been sneaking around even more than normal. I just hope Alfie can keep the secrets of Sibuna far away from Jerome's schemes.

16

The next day in school, Alfie was struggling to put his belongings in his backpack when Jerome spotted him and ran over. "What are you doing? What's that in your bag?" he asked. He snatched Alfie's bag and took out his puzzle piece. "This is one of the puzzle pieces, isn't it?" he said, then put it in his own bag and ran off down the hall. "Sorry, Alfie, I'm going to have to borrow this," he shouted over his shoulder. "Better work on those reflexes for next time. I just need to show Rufus something. Anything!"

"No, Jerome, please give it back!" wailed Alfie as Jerome disappeared into the distance.

Jerome hastily set up a meeting with Rufus and arrived with the stolen puzzle piece. Rufus took it with a pleased smile. "At last. One of the relics. It has been a long wait." He patted Jerome on the back. "You've done well. Now I need you to find the rest of these," he said as he put the piece into his bag.

"You can't keep the puzzle piece! If they realize it's gone, they'll know I'm on to them!" said Jerome, panicking.

"Not my problem. Call me when you have the others, or else!" Rufus stalked away, leaving Jerome more terrified than ever.

Alfie was lounging on his bed listening to music when Jerome returned. Crestfallen, Jerome explained how Rufus had kept the piece, and worse, had demanded more. "I'm sorry. The guy scares me. I had to give him something, Alfie. I had to!" Jerome said.

Although Alfie was furious, he actually felt sorry for Jerome and what he had done to himself.

"Five, six, seven, eight." Victor counted the steps on the staircase. Using an Egyptology book, he had looked up the symbols on the back of Sarah's portrait and guessed that something was hidden beneath the eighth stair. He reached the stair, which had a loose floorboard. "It's all making sense now. Oh yes," he muttered grimly to himself.

❧

Fabian lay on his bed reading an Egyptology book given to him by his uncle Aide. "Unlocking the eye," he muttered to himself. The tear-shaped puzzle piece lay next to him. Fabian picked it up and absentmindedly pressed the gold circle at the bottom of the tear a few times. Suddenly, there was a click, and the puzzle piece fanned out and curved into a bowl made up of tear-shaped petals. He stared at it. "Whoa! That was unexpected," he thought.

Just then, Fabian's roommate, Mick, burst in. "Stop hiding yourself away and come to supper," he said, playfully throwing a football at Fabian. The ball missed and smashed Fabian's favorite mug.

"Now look what you've done! Just get out, Mick," Fabian groaned. As he began picking up the pieces of the mug, a glimmer of understanding entered his brain. He held the now bowl-shaped puzzle piece in one hand, glanced at the page in the book he was studying, and looked at the pieces of the broken mug in his other hand. "Of course!" he exclaimed. He grabbed his book, the puzzle pieces, and some of the broken mug and hurried off to find Nina.

Nina was eating dinner when Fabian ran in and grabbed her by the arm. "Come with me," he said as he whisked her off to his room. He showed Nina a page in his Egyptology book. "Look at this. According to the legend, Anubis was so angry with Amneris for hiding the Cup of Ankh in the tomb, he struck it seven times. SEVEN! And look at this picture here. The Cup was broken into seven pieces." Fabian started to manipulate the mug that Mick had broken. "It's not easy," he said, "but it is possible to put this mug back together."

Realization slowly dawned on Nina's face. "Are you saying that our puzzle pieces are actually the broken pieces of the Cup of Ankh?"

"Yes. That's exactly what I'm saying. Especially when you look at this." Fabian took from his pocket the puzzle piece that had transformed into a bowl.

"Wow!" exclaimed Nina. "So we have the Cup— and we just didn't realize it?"

Fabian nodded excitedly. He pressed the center

of the bowl piece to make it go back to its original teardrop shape.

Nina gasped. "Fantastic work, Fabian! We need to try to put the Cup together. Let's call a Sibuna meeting for tomorrow morning."

17

Dappled light fell through the trees behind Anubis House. Deep in the woods, the Sibuna members gathered next to the lightning-struck tree where they had first become a club.

Nina began. "Fabian and I have this theory we want to try out. We think all the pieces fit together to form the Cup of Ankh. If we all get our pieces out, we can try to make the Cup, right here, right now."

"Awesome theory!" said Patricia. Everyone was really excited except Alfie, who looked like he had seen a ghost. They all handed over the pieces until it was Alfie's turn. He turned a funny color and looked like he was going to vomit. Finally, he blurted out the truth.

"I haven't got my Ankh piece anymore. I showed it to Jerome and he gave it to Rufus."

The others were dumbstruck.

"Alfie! How could you? And who told Jerome about Rufus?" wailed Patricia.

Alfie shook his head. "Jerome knows lots of stuff, and I don't know how." The gang stood there, bewildered. "So what do we do now?" he asked.

Patricia raised her chin. "We are going to find Jerome and make him get the puzzle piece back from Rufus."

The Sibuna members cornered Jerome in his bedroom and asked him about the puzzle piece. Jerome told them he'd had no choice. "Rufus was going to mummify me if I didn't give him something!"

After discussing the situation, the Sibuna members agreed to protect Jerome from Rufus if he could get the puzzle piece back. Once he agreed, they quickly came up with a plan. His hands shaking, Jerome picked up his cell phone and called Rufus.

"I have the rest of the puzzle pieces for you," he said when Rufus picked up. He explained that he needed the puzzle piece he'd given to Rufus in order to access a secret passage that led to the rest of the pieces.

"Victor's out for the night, so I'll sneak down and open the front door after lights-out. Everyone else will be in bed," Jerome said.

"How many pieces are there?" asked Rufus.

"Seven," said Jerome.

"Yes!" said Rufus gleefully. "'And Anubis smote the Cup and the Cup shattered into seven pieces.' I knew it."

"So, I'll see you tonight, then? Midnight?" Jerome squeaked.

"Midnight."

Rufus arrived at exactly midnight. Jerome let him in and led him to the secret passage to the cellar. Although he was suspicious, Rufus handed Jerome the puzzle piece. Jerome pressed the puzzle piece against the secret door, pretending to unlock it, then pushed the door open.

Rufus leaned forward and took a look at the dark passage below. "Intriguing," he murmured. He turned to Jerome and pushed him into the passage. "After you."

The Sibuna members were watching in the

shadows from the next room. Nina had opened the secret passageway with her locket and had planned to close it as soon as Rufus had gone down into the cellar.

"Jerome wasn't supposed to go into the cellar with Rufus," whispered Fabian.

"I can't lock them both in there!" Nina whispered as they ran into the kitchen.

"This is bad. Very bad," said Alfie. "When Rufus realizes there are no other puzzle pieces down there, he's going to mummify Jerome!"

Fabian spoke up. "I say we carry on with the plan as if it's just Rufus down there. Alfie, you slam the front door. Amber and Patricia—alert Victor. Nina, you stay hidden. If Jerome comes out and you get a chance to lock Rufus in there—*do it!*"

"Sibuna!" everyone chimed before running to their positions.

Down in the cellar, Rufus was fascinated by Victor's workbench, which had been turned into an altar. "So this is where the Society meets now," he said. He rummaged around and found the vial of

Victor's Elixir. He took several gulps. When he was done, he wiped his mouth and turned to Jerome. "Where are the other Ankh pieces?" he demanded.

"Well, you see, what happened was . . . ," spluttered Jerome, more frightened than ever.

Just then, Alfie slammed the front door of the house, and Amber and Patricia ran to tell Victor they thought they had heard an intruder.

"What was that?" said Rufus.

"It's Victor; he must be back early," Jerome said, relieved that Victor was coming. Rufus grabbed Jerome and slunk into the shadows. The cellar door creaked open. Victor switched on the lights and crept down the stairs. He crossed over to his workbench and immediately noticed that it had been disturbed.

"Who's there?" he shouted at the shadows.

Rufus emerged, leaving Jerome behind. "Hello, Victor," he said. "So sorry I can't stay and chat, but thanks for the drink." Rufus waved the half-empty Elixir vial in Victor's face.

Jerome knew it was his only chance to escape, so he made a dash for the secret passageway. When he reached the kitchen, Nina pulled him out. She grabbed her locket and moved to shut the secret door.

"Lock him in, quick!" yelled Jerome.

Suddenly, a hand reached out and grabbed Nina. Rufus had rushed after Jerome and now had Nina in a viselike grip.

Rufus flung Nina backward and pushed past her, running into the hall. Victor burst out of the cellar and collided with him. "Not so fast!" Victor yelled as he grabbed Rufus roughly by the collar and wrestled the Elixir out of Rufus's hands. The two men struggled before Rufus broke away and dashed out the door.

Victor chased after Rufus but returned a moment later, disheveled and exhausted. He locked the front door and turned to face the frightened Sibuna members. "We had an intruder, who has now gone. There is no need to call the authorities. So get to bed *now,* all of you."

Dear Diary,

As much as I dislike Jerome, he really saved the day today. He got the puzzle piece back from Rufus after being shoved into the cellar, and Victor nearly caught him. When he returned the piece to us, he asked if Sibuna would continue to protect him from Rufus.

I told him that we had a deal, and if he held up his end of the bargain, we would hold up ours. Jerome then said that if Sibuna didn't protect him, he would go to Victor and the teachers and tell them everything he knew—about the Ankh pieces and our club.

Jerome is NOT one of my favorite people.

18

The next morning, Jerome was the last one down to breakfast. Patricia confronted him immediately. "You need to speak to Rufus again. Play him along. It's the only way of stopping him from coming after us."

Jerome wanted nothing to do with Rufus and quickly tried to change the subject. "Maybe we should have another go at putting those pieces together," he suggested.

"We're going to—tonight. But let's figure out what to do with Rufus," said Nina. The Sibuna members huddled together to devise a new plan.

After school, Jerome mentally rehearsed his story, then took a deep breath and marched over to meet Rufus. When Rufus appeared, he demanded to know why Jerome hadn't helped him the night before.

Jerome paused, thinking wildly. The question wasn't part of the rehearsed plan. "I didn't want Victor to see me and link me to you, so I ran. I thought you were right behind me, to be honest," he lied.

When Rufus asked him for the puzzle piece, Jerome refused to hand it over. "I need to keep it to open the cellar and grab the other Ankh pieces," he explained.

Rufus nodded, but he warned Jerome to act soon. "According to legend, the god Anubis told Amneris that at a certain hour, on a certain day, just once every twenty-five years, a descendant from the bloodline of Amneris is given the opportunity to restore the Cup to its former strength and glory."

"And when's the next date that the Cup can be restored?" asked Jerome.

Rufus suddenly realized he had said too much. "Enough," he said. "Get those pieces for me. And the Elixir. I need the Elixir. Do it, and you'll be well rewarded. I promise."

Jerome sat on Amber's bed as Nina laid out all the

puzzle pieces. "It won't work," he said.

"Will you just shut up or leave the room?" Nina said angrily.

"We have to try, Jerome," said Alfie.

"I'm telling you, you'll never do it. . . ." Jerome smirked.

As Fabian, Nina, Patricia, and Alfie tried to put the Cup together, the house began to shake and groan. All of a sudden, the pieces glowed white, too hot to hold. Jerome simply laughed. "I told you it wouldn't work. I'll tell you what, if you let me into your stupid little club and tell me all your secrets, I'll tell you everything I know. Everything Rufus told me. I will even hold up my side of the bargain first. The reason why you can't assemble the Cup is because it's not the right time. According to Rufus, the Cup can only be assembled on a special date. Once every twenty-five years. And the date is coming up very soon."

"Soon? You got anything a little more specific?" asked Nina.

"Nope, not a clue," Jerome responded merrily. He stood. "Well, guys, better hurry up and get ready for school, or you'll be late!" he called as he strolled out of Nina's room.

Jerome was on his way to class when suddenly Rufus grabbed him and pulled him behind a tree. "Rufus! Ever heard of the phone?" said Jerome, trying to hide his terror.

"I need those Ankh pieces. And soon," said Rufus.

Jerome swallowed hard. "Look, if you would tell me when this special date is, I'd know what my deadline is, and then I could—"

Rufus suddenly snapped. He pushed Jerome up against the tree. "Don't play me for a fool!" he roared. "How about this for a deadline? Tomorrow morning! I get those puzzle pieces in my hand by tomorrow morning; otherwise you're the one who's dead. Is that deadline enough for you?"

Rufus released his grip and Jerome fell in a heap on the ground. "Tomorrow. Or else!" Rufus warned, and walked off.

Jerome darted back to the house and ran up to Nina's room. He searched frantically through her belongings for the puzzle pieces. His fear of Rufus had overcome his loyalty to Sibuna.

"What do you think you're doing?" demanded

Nina, entering her room just as Jerome found a puzzle piece. "Don't you dare move. I'm calling the others."

Once everyone had gathered, Nina said to Jerome, "I thought you wanted to be a Sibuna member."

"I did. I mean, I do. But you don't understand. Rufus threatened me! And this time, he really, really meant it," Jerome said.

There was a pause. Alfie shrugged. "So what happens now?"

Fabian took the lead. "Okay, let's try to find out when this 'special date' is and take it from there. If we can keep protecting the Ankh pieces until after this special date has passed, then maybe we'll be in the clear."

"For another twenty-five years, at least," Patricia added.

Nina reached under her bed and pulled out the box Sarah had given her. "Maybe there's a clue in here about the date," she said. She opened the box and gave each Sibuna member an object to look at.

After a few minutes, Fabian cleared his throat. "Guys. I think I might have found something. Look at this. It's a star map." He turned the map around.

"I don't recognize these constellations, but I'm going online to check it out." He took the map and dashed out of the room. Nina ran after him.

"I'm coming too," she said.

Fabian went to his room and got his laptop. After half an hour of browsing, he spoke up. "Okay. It's definitely an Ancient Egyptian star map. This is the constellation of Osiris, and that one there is Isis. But what do these here mean?" he asked, pointing to some numbers on the map.

"Coordinates?" suggested Nina.

Fabian snapped his fingers. "Of course! Latitude and longitude." He bit his lip and leaned forward, studying the information he had just found.

Nina smiled. "I love that funny little frown you get when you're concentrating."

Fabian turned to Nina. Their eyes met.

Patricia burst through the door, interrupting the romantic moment. "Guys, get this. Jerome just told us that the Cup of Ankh can only be put together by the Chosen One. By Joy! I have to call her and warn her. Do we know the date?"

"Not yet, but I think when this constellation lines up with these coordinates . . . ," Fabian said as he tapped furiously on his keyboard. "Yes!" The star map on his screen shifted slightly as the constellation lined up with the coordinates. "We've got our date and time. This Friday. Midnight."

Patricia grinned. "We have the Ankh pieces. We know the date. We know who the Chosen One is. We can put the Cup together and end our search!"

As the Sibuna members gathered around and congratulated one another, they didn't notice a shadowy figure lurking outside the door. In the hallway, Victor smiled to himself. "Who would have thought that after all these years, simply eaves- dropping at a bedroom door would solve all my problems?" he mused. He took his ear from the door and scurried down the corridor.

Dear Diary,

We're nearly at the end of the mystery! At midnight this Friday we're going to put the Cup of Ankh together. Crazily enough, Friday is also the day of the school prom. I'm going with Fabian, and Patricia's roommate, Mara, is going with Mick. Amber and Patricia are going alone, but I'll make sure they have a great time. Wouldn't it be wonderful if Sibuna solved the mystery and I got a kiss from Fabian on the same night?

19

"They know that Joy is the Chosen One. They have pinpointed the Chosen Hour, and most importantly—they have all the Ankh pieces," Victor said to Mr. Sweet, Jason Winkler, and Mrs. Andrews, "which is what Rufus was probably looking for when he broke in."

Mr. Sweet suggested they carry out another search of the rooms, but Victor told him they should sit back and let the Cup come to them.

"How do you mean?" asked Jason.

"They're in touch with Joy. So we speak to her father. He can check her phone for messages. Keep an eye on her. Find out what they're planning," Victor explained.

The night of the prom arrived. In Anubis House, everyone was getting ready. Trudy was just answering the door to a deliveryman when Mara and Amber came down the stairs. Trudy called out, "Amber, delivery."

Amber rushed to the door, signed for the package, and began ripping it open. "Yes! Finally. Thank you thank you thank you thank you." Alfie and Jerome watched from the hallway as Amber pulled a tiny dress out of the package.

"Amber, that's a doll's dress," Mara said.

Amber held the dress up against herself. "I ordered a doll's dress for the prom?" She stood perplexed for a second. Then she let out a wail and ran up the stairs.

Jerome beckoned Alfie to follow him, and they went to their room. Inside, Jerome laughed hysterically as he held up Amber's real dress. "Amber's face! 'I ordered a doll's dress?'" he mimicked cruelly.

"You took the real one?" Alfie asked, fiddling with his cuff links.

"Yup, arrived yesterday." Jerome cocked his head at Alfie's look of disapproval. "Well, I had to take my mind off Rufus somehow. I can't wait to see what kind of fancy dress Amber can scrounge from the other girls. It's either geek, Goth, or Goody Two-shoes."

As Jerome turned to the mirror to put on his tie, Alfie picked up the dress and ran out of the room. He ran past Fabian in the hallway just as Nina, Patricia, and Mara entered. They had their prom dresses on and looked gorgeous. But Patricia was carrying a large leather bag that didn't match her outfit.

Amber was lying on her bed, crying into her pillow, when she heard a small noise. She sat up and saw Alfie, who had grabbed a silver wand and a tiara from her dresser and was waving them over her head. She giggled. "Alfie, what are you doing?"

"Do not fear, Amberella. You shall go to the ball!" Alfie replied as he presented her dress from behind his back. "And before you jump to conclusions, it wasn't me who stole your real dress. It was Jerome," he said.

Amber got to her feet and took the dress. "Oh, Alfie," she said. "Thank you. You've saved the prom." She gave Alfie a big hug, but then sat down again. "Shame I haven't got a date, though."

Alfie got up the courage to ask Amber to the prom.

Amber smiled at Alfie and accepted. "Now go wait downstairs. I have six hours of beautifying to squeeze into five minutes," she said, laughing, and hustled the beaming Alfie out of the room.

As the Anubis House pupils waited for Amber to come downstairs, Trudy joined them. "You all look so grown-up and beautiful," she gushed. "Where's Amber?" she asked just as Amber appeared at the top of the stairs in her dress. She looked fantastic.

The students headed to the school, where the prom was being held. As they entered, the Sibuna members decided to find a quiet place to discuss how they were going to assemble the Ankh pieces. They headed into an empty classroom away from the prom and ran into Jason there, dressed in his tuxedo.

"Oh, hello. Why you aren't at the dance?" he asked.

"Why aren't you?" Patricia replied suspiciously.

Jason told them he was waiting for his date.

Suddenly, the classroom door burst open and Rufus rushed in. He was holding an ornate Egyptian hourglass. Tiny red flies buzzed around inside.

"I'll take that," Rufus said, grabbing Patricia's oversized bag. Jason moved toward him. "Don't even think about it," snarled Rufus. He waved the hourglass and the flies buzzed angrily. "These are red Sutekh sand flies. They are very rare, quite vicious, and certainly deadly." He thrust the hourglass toward Jason. "You. Bring me the Chosen One and the Elixir. If I don't have both within the hour, I will smash the hourglass."

"You're insane," Jason replied, horrified.

"Very observant," sneered Rufus. "Now go!"

Jason left, and Rufus locked the door behind him. He snatched Patricia's bag and opened it. He had expected to find the Ankh pieces, but he pulled out a bottle of water instead. "What is this?" he demanded.

Rufus pulled bottle after bottle out of the bag. He became increasingly enraged as Alfie, Fabian, and Jerome looked quizzically at Patricia and Nina. "Where are my Ankh pieces? You'll all pay for this!" Rufus screamed.

"Did you really think we'd be stupid enough to keep the pieces with us today of all days, knowing everyone is after them?" Nina replied. Rufus didn't answer. He lifted the hourglass high.

Meanwhile, Joy had snuck out of the place where her father was keeping her. Patricia had texted her and said the Sibuna members would join her at eleven p.m. to assemble the Cup of Ankh. She told Joy to look for the Ankh pieces inside a hollowed-out tree behind Anubis House. Joy found the tree and hunted around. Hidden in the hollow was a bag that looked identical to Patricia's. Joy took a quick look in the bag. The Ankh pieces were there! She smiled and settled down to wait. The minutes ticked by, and she grew anxious. It was almost midnight. The Sibuna members were very late.

Suddenly, Joy's father, Victor, Mr. Sweet, and Mrs. Andrews appeared and surrounded her.

"Don't look so scared, baby. You're not in trouble," Joy's dad said gently. "But you do need to come with us now."

Victor chuckled. "Thought you'd given your father the slip, didn't you? Instead you were leading us . . . to these," he said as he picked up the bag and pulled out the Ankh pieces.

A reluctant Joy was taken to Anubis House and led down to the cellar. Just then, there was a knock at the door. Victor answered it, and Nurse Delia and Sergeant Roebuck entered.

Just as Victor was ushering them into the cellar, Jason arrived at the door. Victor went back up the stairs.

"Victor," Jason said, gasping for breath. "At last! I've been looking everywhere for you. We have a problem. Rufus Zeno is holding the children captive in one of the classrooms, and he's threatening to harm them unless he gets what he wants."

Victor smiled. "So much the better. If Rufus is holding the children captive, he won't get in our way."

"We can't just leave them!" cried Jason.

Victor loomed over him. "What is the nature of your medical condition again, Mr. Winkler? It's a degenerative illness, isn't it?" he said pointedly. "And just think. Eternal life could free you of all your suffering."

Jason slumped, his resolve broken. Victor put his hand on Jason's shoulder and guided him down the stairs. "The gods have chosen us to receive their gift. The best thing we can do is complete the ceremony and then deal with Zeno," he said as they descended into the cellar.

Dozens of bloodred candles cast an eerie yellow glow. Dressed in their elaborate ceremonial robes, the Society members gathered in a circle. Joy stood, terrified, in the center of the circle, next to an altar for the jackal god Anubis. She wore a hooded robe of pure white. Victor read from an ancient scroll as the adults walked around Joy.

"'And so the seven followers of Ankh shall sip the Elixir of Life from the Cup. And the Scales of Life will be tipped. Strength and life will flow into them from seven young acolytes, and thus death is conquered.'" He turned to Joy. "Step forward, Chosen One."

"What was that about the seven young acolytes?" Joy asked, alarmed.

"They are merely represented by these coins," Victor responded, and gestured to the seven sets of weighing scales. On one side of each of the scales was a coin bearing a name—Joy's name, and the names of each of the Sibuna members. On the other side of each of the scales was a coin bearing the name of one of the Society members.

"Just do it, darling. It'll be okay," Joy's dad said.

Joy stepped forward. The seven puzzle pieces were in front of her on the altar. She started to put them together.

In the classroom, Rufus was pacing around the room, contemplating his next move. A clock struck midnight, and the Sibuna members breathed a sigh of relief. The Chosen Hour had passed, and the Cup could not be assembled for another twenty-five years. Fabian told Rufus it was over and that he should let the students go.

"It's not over until the full hour itself is over," Rufus snapped. "They're probably putting the Cup together as we speak. You're all still alive. So they clearly haven't drunk from it yet."

The students were aghast. "Run that by me again," Nina said.

"Oh yes. Victor and the others think it's just symbolic. The tipping of the scales. The symbolic flowing of life force from the young to the old. But immortality comes at a price."

"And by price, you mean . . . ?" Nina asked with a growing sense of horror.

"It's a life for a life, my dear," Rufus said, and began to laugh.

Nina was terrified as she worked out the implications of what Rufus had said. She turned to Fabian. "Those coins with our names on them in Victor's office. The scales . . . if Joy puts the Cup together, we're going to die!"

Rufus laughed grimly. "I still have time to relieve Victor of the Cup, if you are all still alive. You," he said, pointing at Nina. "You're coming with me. The rest of you . . . prepare to say good night! Forever!"

He waved the hourglass at them again. Amber began to scream as Rufus pulled Nina to her feet and tried to drag her to the door. Fabian jumped up and tackled Rufus from behind, screaming, "Leave her!"

Rufus tumbled and the hourglass went sailing into the air toward Alfie.

Alfie leapt forward. He dived and caught the hourglass an inch from the ground. Terrified, he tossed it to Nina.

In the confusion, Jerome was able to unlock the door, and everyone scrambled toward it. As Rufus staggered to his feet, the students fled the classroom. Nina and Jerome were the last to leave.

"Throw the hourglass. Throw it!" Jerome ordered Nina.

"I can't!" Nina replied.

Jerome grabbed the hourglass out of Nina's hands and threw it into the classroom. It smashed open on the floor. Rufus writhed in agony as the flies attacked. Jerome slammed the door.

Jerome and Nina ran to catch up with the others, who had gathered near the lockers. Nina ran straight into Fabian's arms.

"You okay?" Fabian asked her tenderly.

Nina nodded, but her eyes were shining with tears as she gestured toward the classroom. "Rufus . . . ," she cried.

"It was him or us, Nina," Jerome said.

Nina told them they had to warn the teachers to not drink from the Cup. "Because if they do, we die."

"There's no need to be scared, it's going to be okay!" said Fabian. But no one was listening. They had sped off toward the cellar.

"It's not working. I can't do it!" wailed Joy as she flung two Ankh pieces down.

"Yes, you can. Say the incantation again," her father encouraged. "With this circle of light . . ."

"With this circle of light, I seal the circle of life," Joy began again, and took up the pieces, but she still had no idea how to assemble the Cup.

Victor was becoming agitated. "Do it, for goodness' sake!" he urged. The other Society members looked increasingly worried.

"I can't!" Joy said. She set the pieces down in defeat.

Victor's shoulders sagged. "It's over."

"The children!" said Jason as he bolted for the door. "They are in danger!" Mr. Sweet and Mrs. Andrews ran up the cellar steps behind Jason.

Nurse Delia and Sergeant Roebuck looked lost and turned to Victor for guidance.

"Victor? What now?" Sergeant Roebuck asked.

"Leave me. Leave me," Victor said. The Society members and Joy departed, leaving Victor to his cold, bleak thoughts.

Joy headed quickly up the stairs just as the Sibuna members burst into the hall. "Patricia. You're safe!" said Joy, hugging her friend. Joy explained that nothing had happened. She was not the Chosen One, and the Cup of Ankh was still in pieces.

Nina hesitated, then spoke up. "They told you being the Chosen One had something to do with your birthday, right?"

"Yeah. The seventh of July," Joy confirmed.

"My birthday's the seventh of July too," Nina said quietly.

"Joy, were you born at seven a.m.?" Fabian asked. "Apparently, the Chosen One was born on the seventh hour on the seventh day of the seventh month."

"No, I was born at seven at night," Joy said.

"Nina?" Fabian asked, his voice breathless.

"I don't know. Sometime in the morning, though," she replied.

"I bet it was seven a.m.—the true seventh hour!" Fabian shouted. "You, Nina, are the Chosen One!" He looked at the clock on the wall. It was a quarter to one. They had fifteen minutes of the Chosen Hour left. "Where are the pieces?" he asked Joy.

"Down in the cellar," she replied.

"Nina?" Fabian said.

Nina was still thinking about it when a gust of wind blew through the hall, rattling the doors and windows. The lights dimmed and came back up again.

Then Nina heard Sarah's voice. It sounded as if it came from a great distance. "Nina, hurry. You don't have long. Make the Cup," said Sarah.

"Let's do this," Nina said, finally making her decision.

While they were talking, Victor had staggered upstairs to his office. The Sibuna members crept down the cellar steps. Nina went to the altar and then hesitated. She was staring at the Ankh pieces, still not sure it was the right thing to do. Then she saw Sarah's face shimmering behind the altar, encouraging her. "You are the Chosen One, Nina. This is your destiny. Make the Cup," Sarah said. Her face faded away, and Nina quickly started to assemble the pieces.

"You have to say the incantation," Joy said. "Say 'With this circle of light, I seal the circle of life.'"

"With this circle of light, I seal the circle of life,"

Nina echoed. With instinct guiding her, she carefully fitted the pieces together. When she was finished, she stepped back. There was silence.

Nina frowned. "Nothing's happening! Why is nothing happening?"

"Nina, look—your locket!" Amber gasped.

Nina looked down. Her locket was glowing brightly. She chanted, "With this circle of light, I seal the circle of life," and held the locket against the Cup. The others gasped as the pieces started to glow brightly. Suddenly, a fiery whirlwind surrounded Nina and the Cup.

"Nina!" Fabian exclaimed. The whirlwind subsided and Nina was left holding a glowing chalice in her hands.

"You did it," Fabian breathed.

"I did," Nina replied, relieved. "And now I have to hide it. For good."

"Not if I have anything to do with it," they heard a sinister voice say.

They turned, aghast to see Rufus, who had sneaked down the cellar steps. His face had been badly stung, but he was very much alive.

Rufus grabbed Amber around the waist. "Did you

really think I'd expose myself to the deadly Sutekh sand fly without first equipping myself with an antidote?" he said. He held up his fist, and they could hear a buzzing fly inside. "And here I have the queen, which I will put in this pretty girl's ear if you don't do exactly as I say," he continued. He looked at Nina. "You. Bring me the Cup." Then he turned to Fabian. "You. Bring me the Elixir from the altar. Quickly. We only have minutes left."

He held his fist close to Amber's cheek, and she screamed as she heard the buzzing so close to her. Reluctantly, Nina and Fabian did as they were told.

From his office, Victor heard Amber screaming. He ran down the stairs to investigate.

Rufus ordered Fabian to pour the Elixir into the Cup. "Every drop," he said.

Fabian did as he was told. Rufus took the Cup. As he raised it to his lips, he pushed Amber to the floor and squashed the sand fly in his palm. Then he drank.

"Finally—eternity is mine!" he cried triumphantly, just as Victor arrived.

"Why, Rufus? Why? We could have all shared this. That was our plan," Victor implored.

Rufus sneered. "No. That was *your* plan, Victor. I always had other ideas. Big ideas I knew you and your pathetic Society would never approve of. And then when I learned the true meaning behind the Scales of Life, I knew it was time to go at it alone." Rufus turned to the students. "Anyone feeling poorly?" he asked.

Alfie said he felt a little dizzy. He started wheezing and loosened his bow tie.

"What are you talking about?" Victor demanded of Rufus. "What's happening?"

Rufus plucked the coin etched with Alfie's name from the scales. "The symbolic flowing of the life force," he said. "It's not symbolic at all, Victor. It really happens. That boy is going to die, and I am going to live forever!"

"No!" Victor cried, and rushed over to where Alfie was now collapsed on the floor. Rufus was laughing maniacally as he threw the Cup into the furnace and ran from the cellar. The others gathered around Alfie, calling out his name in panic.

"Guys. Listen up," Fabian began.

"Please, please, let him live. I'll do anything," Amber sobbed.

"Guys!" Fabian continued.

"Anything?" Alfie gasped. "Like . . . be my girlfriend, even?"

"Of course, Alfie—anything, anything," Amber said.

"GUYS!" Fabian said loudly, finally getting their attention. "Alfie, you can stop acting now."

"What?" Nina cried. "Fabian. You know what happens when someone drinks the Elixir from the Cup of Ankh."

"Except Rufus didn't drink the Elixir. He's not immortal." Everyone looked at Fabian in shock, waiting for an explanation. He looked at Patricia and Nina and began. "You remember your little insurance policy—having the two identical bags, letting Joy look after the pieces? Well, I had my own little insurance policy, but I couldn't tell anyone because I didn't trust Jerome." Fabian explained that he had saved some of the fake Elixir that Alfie had drunk a week before. He had taken the spare cellar key from Victor's office. He had then gone down to the cellar, tipped away the real Elixir, and replaced it with the fake herbal liquid.

Victor groaned. "You threw the Elixir away?" His

shoulders sagged as he stumbled up the cellar steps.

Nina threw her arms around Fabian's neck. "You're a genius, Fabian. I love you!" The two shared an awkward special moment.

Amber asked if that meant Alfie wasn't really dying.

Alfie grinned. "I did actually feel a bit ill for a second."

The Sibuna gang finally headed to the prom. "Guess it's all over, then," Fabian said.

"Guess so," Nina replied.

Fabian held out his hand. Nina took it, then hesitated and stepped back. She swore she could hear Sarah's voice telling her to go back into the cellar.

"You go on. I'll see you over there," she told him.

As the other Sibuna members left, Nina went back into the cellar. She looked around, and Sarah appeared to her in a vision. "Take the Cup," said Sarah.

Nina took the Cup, undamaged from the suddenly cold furnace. The ghosts of Sarah's mother and father appeared on either side of her and placed their hands on the Cup alongside Sarah's. "The Cup has been restored. The curse can be lifted. We can rest in peace. Now take it. Hide it. Make it safe," Sarah said.

Nina took the Cup from Sarah. The three ghosts shimmered and disappeared.

"Where've you been? I was worried," Fabian asked as Nina arrived at the prom, looking disheveled but happy.

"Just taking care of something," she replied.

The music suddenly stopped and Amber made an announcement. She told the crowd that that it was time to announce the prom king and queen. As the student body had not had a chance to organize a vote, she had made the decision herself. "The prom king is Fabian Rutter!" she said.

Fabian was shocked. Alfie pushed him toward Amber, and she placed a makeshift crown on his head. "And the prom queen is Nina Martin!" she said. Amber plunked the crown on Nina's head. Then she said, "Now dance, you two."

A slow song started to play, and Fabian and Nina danced. Everyone applauded and joined in.

"That was embarrassing," Nina said to Fabian.

Fabian smiled shyly. "Very. You look . . ."

"Ridiculous," Nina finished.

Fabian shook his head. "I was going to say beautiful. So, will you tell me where you were?"

"Did you just call me beautiful?" Nina asked, smiling.

"Yes. So come on. Where were you?" he asked again.

"All that can wait. This can't," she answered as she leaned closer to him. Finally, they kissed.

Everyone in the room cheered. The music changed to an upbeat song, and everyone was up and dancing. Fabian and Nina were oblivious as they gazed happily into each other's eyes.

In a space underneath the stage, hidden from view, the Cup glowed brightly. It was safe. For now . . .

Dear Diary,

My head is spinning! We made the Cup of Ankh and stopped Victor and Rufus—and Fabian and I are now officially a couple! I feel like the luckiest girl in the world. Solving the mystery of Anubis House really brought Sibuna together. I know that Fabian, Amber, Alfie, Patricia, Joy, and I are going to be friends forever.

Well, Fabian might be more than just a friend.

It's three in the morning and I should get to bed. I'm going to sleep well tonight—and so will Sarah and her parents. Their curse has been lifted. May they rest in peace. Sibuna!